W9-AKD-221

3 4028 09403 1169
HARRIS COUNTY PUBLIC LIBRARY

J Clowe
Clowe, Amberly Kristen
Teeny Sweeney and the
    mustache cash

$7.99
on1037009421

First edition.

on1037009421

Teeny Sweeney and the Mustache Cash

Written by
Amberly Kristen Clowe

Illustrations by Janet Samuel

WITHDRAWN

little lamb
BOOKS

Teeny Sweeney and the Mustache Cash
Text copyright © 2018 Amberly Kristen Clowe
Illustrations copyright © 2018 Janet Samuel
ISBN: 978-0-9986243-6-5 (Hardcover)
ISBN: 978-0-9986243-4-1 (Paperback)
ISBN: 9978-0-9986243-7-2 (eBook)
Library of Congress Control Number: 2017963206

little lamb
BOOKS

Published by Little Lamb Books
www.littlelambbooks.com
P.O. Box 211724, Bedford, TX 76021

No part of this book may be used or reproduced in any manner
whatsoever without written permission except in the case of
brief quotation embodied in critical articles and reviews.

Scriptures taken from the Holy Bible, New International Version, NIV.
Copyright ©1973, 1978, 1984, 2011 by Biblica, Inc. Used by permission of
Zondervan. All rights reserved worldwide. *www.zondervan.com*
The NIV and New International Version are trademarks registered in the
United States Patent and Trademark Office by Biblica, Inc.

Written by Amberly Kristen Clowe, *amberlykristenclowe.com*
Illustrations by Janet Samuel, *thebrightagency.com*
Edited by Lindsay Schlegel, *lindsayschlegel.com*
Design by Monica Thomas for TLC Book Design, *TLCBookDesign.com*
Pecan praline recipe courtesy of Rose Atwater,
owner of Rose Bakes, *rosebakes.com*

First Edition
Printed in the USA

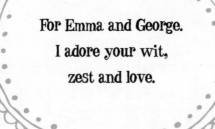

For Emma and George.
I adore your wit,
zest and love.

Contents

Chapter 1

Not the Sparkle Marker

"This will be our most exciting assignment yet." Miss Powl grabbed her lucky marker from the big apple on the corner of her desk.

Teeny leaned toward the red-headed boy in front of her. "She said that last time, and the time before that," Teeny whispered to Garrett, her best friend since kindergarten.

"*Shhhh*, Teeny. I'm not getting in trouble again, because you talk too—"

"Garrett, is there something you'd like to share with the rest of the class?" Miss Powl stopped at the bottom curl of the last *s* in the word *Business*. She wasn't even facing the class.

How does she always do that? thought Teeny.

"Sorry, Miss Powl." Garrett slumped in his seat.

Teeny would get an earful about that later.

Miss Powl turned to the class, the words *Business Plan* on the white board behind her. She had the prettiest handwriting of all the third-grade teachers.

"This assignment will complete our Economics unit." Miss Powl smiled at her classroom full of students. She took a deep breath.

Teeny nervously flipped her pencil back and forth between her fingers. Miss Powl only took deep breaths when something was major.

"Has anyone ever heard of a *business plan*?" Miss Powl walked from the world map on one side of the room to the multiplication facts poster on the other.

Not a single person raised his hand. Teeny could almost hear the snot bubbles popping from Mark Klenton's nose six desks behind her.

"That's okay." Miss Powl laced her fingers together. "Let's start smaller. What is a business?"

A single hand lifted into the air faster than all the others. Of course, it belonged to Amanda Mayweather.

"Yes, Amanda."

Amanda flipped one of her blonde pigtails behind her shoulder. "A business is a person, partnership, or corporation engaged in commerce, manufacturing, or a service."

"Very good," said Miss Powl. Amanda smiled smugly. Teeny squeezed her pencil so hard, it snapped. She unzipped her pencil bag and put it with all the others.

"But I was hoping for a definition in your own words," said Miss Powl.

Before Teeny could stop herself, she laughed.

Miss Powl's eyes narrowed. "Tina, would you please define the word *business* in your own words?"

Most days, this was when Teeny stalled by clearing her throat, but not today. "My parents both own businesses. My mom grooms pets, and my dad drives a food truck. He's the best cook I know."

"Okay, that's a start. Now, can you tell me what a business is in your own words?"

The answer came to Teeny faster than a June bug to a porch light—even faster than Amanda's usual know-it-all answers. "A business is something that you do to make money."

Miss Powl walked to the second row of desks. She stopped in front of Teeny's nametag, the most doodled-on cardstock in the room. "Very well put, Tina."

As Miss Powl turned back to the board, Teeny found Amanda glaring at her. Teeny stuck out her tongue.

"Class, your assignment is to create a business plan. This is a plan to make money. Go ahead and write this down. You're going to need it."

The class gave a collective groan—all except for Teeny and Amanda.

Miss Powl wrote a small checkmark beneath the title and the question *Why*. "Why start a business? Why is it needed?" She wrote another check and the word *Different*. "Second, how is your business different than other businesses? You will need it to stand out, to be unique." She wrote a third check and the words *Product or Service*. "What will you make or do to earn money?"

Teeny thought her heart would explode at any moment. Finally, an assignment that didn't make her want to run, screaming for the nearest exit.

Miss Powl wrote another check and the word *Audience*. "Who will buy your product or service? Give this quite a bit of detail. The more you know

about your audience, the more you know what it is they want.

"And finally," Miss Powl wrote her last check and the word *Numbers*. "How much will your product cost to create? If customers are paying for a service, how much will it cost for you to complete the service? How much will you charge for the product or service? What profit, or money, will you make?"

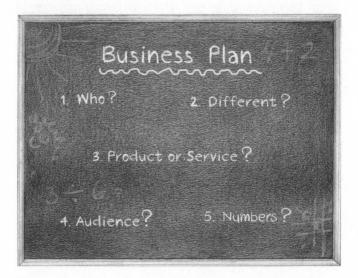

Miss Powl snapped the lid back on her marker. "Today is Friday. I will give you one week to create your business plan. We will present next Friday. Remember, this is just a plan. You won't actually have a business or spend or make money. So please, be creative. The sky is the limit."

The final bell rang. Notebooks slammed and chairs screeched as kids leaped up.

"Make sure to let me know by Monday what your family will bring for the bake sale next Saturday. We want our third-grade booth to sell the most. Remember, whichever grade makes the most money gets an ice cream party."

The room exploded in cheers. Teeny's grade was the one to beat, and the entire school knew it. They had won every year since kindergarten.

But who can think of ice cream, Teeny thought, *when I get to create a business!*

Chapter 2

Earth to Zane

"For the last time, quit talking to me during class, Teeny." Garrett pulled tighter on his backpack straps.

"You know Miss Powl already sent a letter home to my mom. If I keep getting in trouble, she's going to put it on my official report card. *Official*, Teeny."

Teeny popped a stick of chewing gum into her mouth. "Got it. Official." She smacked her gum as loud as she could. "Let's get down to business." Teeny winked.

"When have you ever been excited about an assignment?" Garrett lifted a hand to her forehead.

She slapped it away. "Since we finally have an assignment worth doing! My parents are the king and queen of business. That makes me business royalty, and I've had the perfect idea for a business since probably before I learned to speak."

Garrett groaned. "I'm afraid to ask."

Teeny ran her hand across the sky. "The Doggie Diner." She paused, waiting for applause. When none came, she continued, "I'll combine the best of both of my parents' worlds: dogs and food."

"Ewww." Garrett's nose crinkled.

Teeny elbowed him in the side. "Not like that. The Doggie Diner will be a fine restaurant, but unlike other fine restaurants, mine will let customers eat alongside their favorite pets. I'm absolutely going to create a better business plan than Amanda Mayweather. You wait. Miss Powl will give me a standing ovation once I'm done."

Amanda walked past Teeny, bumping her shoulder. "The Doggie Diner? It's called Bella's Best Friends, and it opened last week. Honestly, I didn't expect much from you, Teeny Sweeney, but stealing someone else's idea and calling it your own? That's low even for you." Amanda flipped a pigtail and turned towards her mom's red SUV parked alongside the curb.

"She's lying! She has to be lying!" Teeny said.

Garrett sunk lower into his shirt. "Well…"

Teeny growled. "*That Amanda Mayweather.*" She squeezed her eyes shut. No one made Teeny angrier than Amanda.

"Don't worry about it." Even when Garrett was mad at Teeny, he still wanted her to be happy. "You'll think of something amazing. You always do."

Garrett waved before walking towards the bus-rider line that was already five people deep. Garrett liked to sit in the front, because Mr. Simmons, the bus driver, let his parrot, Saltine,

ride on his shoulder. Garrett had taught Saltine to say, "Third-graders rock" and "Garrett's the best."

As the Mayweather SUV pulled away, the Sweeney Sheen van took its place at the curb. Snickers erupted throughout the school grounds. Every time her mom picked her up, it was the same thing. *By now*, thought Teeny, *shouldn't the other kids be used to pointy cat ears sprouting from a car roof and giant whiskers poking out from a bumper?*

Teeny yanked open the back door. She threw her backpack across the seat. "Floor it, Mom. Let's get out of here!"

"Hey, cool it with the *Mom* stuff, Teens," Teeny's big brother Zane called over his shoulder.

"Where's Mom?" Teeny buckled herself into the seat.

"She had an emergency grooming at the house, something about a cocker spaniel competition. Who knows." Zane tossed Teeny a juice packet. "Here, kid."

"Thanks." Teeny stabbed the packet with a straw. "Zane, have you heard of Bella's Best Friends?" Teeny paused for a few slurps.

"Sure. Jen Lankton's already been there with her poodle."

"That was my idea. Zane, that should have been my restaurant!"

Silence filled the van.

"Hello, Earth to Zane." Teeny waved at the rearview mirror.

Zane rubbed his hand over the sides of his face and then beneath his nose. "Teeny, it's just some place to eat. I've got real problems here. I'd spend my last dime for a little facial hair, just a simple mustache. *Anything.*"

"You don't even have a dime." Teeny huffed. "And besides, your face looks fine."

"Fine. *Fine?* I don't want to look *fine,* Teeny. Jen Lankton doesn't date guys who look *fine.*" Zane glimpsed at his little sister in the rearview

mirror. He sighed. "Never mind. Let's go. Dad's making chicken Parmesan tonight."

It used to be great that Zane was seven years older than Teeny. When she was four and he was eleven, they built forts and played good guys and bad guys all day. He would even buy Teeny ice cream from the neighborhood ice cream truck. They'd laugh and eat while it melted all over the curb at the front of their house.

But this new, older Zane, the one with the driver's license who wouldn't let Teeny hang out with him and his friends, who seemed annoyed every time Teeny spoke to him? Teeny didn't know this guy at all.

The blinker ticked as Zane pulled away from the school slower than a tortoise. He wasn't even a very good driver compared to their parents. Teeny had never thought much about driving, but if it meant changing like her brother, she never wanted to get behind the wheel.

The clock ticked way faster than the blinker, and Teeny's brain went into overdrive. She needed the perfect idea to make Amanda Mayweather look anything but perfect.

Chapter 3

Boomin' Groomin'

"Mom? Mom!" Teeny tossed her backpack against the backdoor. She hurried through the living room and down the hall. When Teeny was five and her mom decided to quit her job with a larger pet company and start The Sweeney Sheen, her parents added a room to the house just for the grooming business.

It was super annoying at times like these, when Teeny needed her mom, like, yesterday.

She finally reached the opened doorway and nearly flew inside. "Mom!"

Teeny's mom hugged her customer close, fluffy curls and all. "Teeny, you know better than to scare the dogs with your yelling. This is their home away from home. They need to feel comfortable. How can they shine if they're frightened?"

Teeny fell into the blue, vinyl chair beside the door. "Mom, I—" She dipped her head between her knees.

Mrs. Sweeney lifted the dog from the metal grooming table to the tiled floor. She grabbed a treat shaped like a t-bone steak from a glass jar and let the dog pluck it from her hand. She reached her daughter in two quick steps. She leaned down, stroking Teeny's long, curly hair. "What's wrong, Teeny? What happened? Are you hurt?"

A big, uncomfortable lump settled smack dab in the middle of Teeny's throat. She raised her head and the words finally croaked themselves out. "It's a business plan, Mom. I thought I would

have this one in the bag. I mean, hello, I've got business in the genes. But Bella's Best Friends ruined everything! This was supposed to be my one fun assignment! Why does it already feel like so much work?"

Mrs. Sweeney's lips pressed together in a firm line. "Tina Michelle Sweeney."

Uh-oh, Teeny thought.

"Did you really rush through this house, yelling like a crazed person and scaring sweet, little Dixie here"—Teeny's mom had already scooped up the four-legged blob of curls and set her back on the grooming table—"fall into that chair as dramatic as a person could, and put your head in your hands—which as you know, always scares me—because of a school assignment?"

"Ouch." Zane strolled into the room. "I told you it wasn't a real problem."

Teeny felt the blood rush to her face. She pushed her foot out to trip Zane, but stopped,

grabbing her nose instead. "Ewww, Zane, you smell gross."

"What?" Her brother shrugged.

"She's right, Zane," Mrs. Sweeney agreed. "What is that smell?"

"Some of the guys said vinegar can help you grow facial hair." Zane stuck his nose beneath the front of his t-shirt. He flinched. "Okay, so, yeah, that is pretty bad." He hurried from the room and pounded through the house.

It wasn't until water began to run in the upstairs bathroom that Teeny and her mom erupted in a fit of laughter. Teeny had to admit she needed that laugh.

Mrs. Sweeney finally sighed. "Teeny, you're right that business plans can be a lot of work, but it's like the Bible says in Proverbs 16:3: 'Commit to the Lord whatever you do, and your plans will succeed.' When you work hard, God will guide you. We're happy to help, too, but next time, try not to scare me half to death. Okay?"

The only sound in the room was Dixie's breathing.

"Okay, Teeny?"

Teeny nodded her head. She'd only half-heard what her mom had said.

She suddenly had the perfect idea for a business, and she had the trashcan full of dog hair in the corner of the room to thank for that.

Chapter 4

Magnificent Creation

"Hey, Dad." Teeny grabbed one of her dad's famous French cheese straws from the tall, glass bowl on the kitchen counter. The puffy bread melted in her mouth.

"Hey!" Mr. Sweeney snatched the dishtowel on his shoulder and pretended to pop Teeny's leg, "I'll call you when everything is ready. Eating a cheese straw without my homemade marinara should be a crime."

Teeny wiggled away and chomped down on the cheesy straw once more before tossing the rest back into the bowl. She giggled as her dad chased her a few more steps. He then returned to the stovetop to stir his red sauce.

"Do you have any double-sided tape?" Teeny asked.

Mr. Sweeney pulled down the stove door and peeked in on the chicken Parmesan. "Double-sided tape, huh? Hmmm… check the everything drawer."

Teeny hurried to the one drawer in the house that seemed to contain everything they all needed, whenever they needed it. She dug through its contents, pushing aside leftover crayons and out-of-date coupons. "Yes!" Teeny pulled out a tape dispenser.

"What do you need the tape for, sweet pea?" Mr. Sweeney asked.

"It's for my busine—"

"*Magnifique!*" Teeny's dad shouted in his best French accent and kissed the tips of his fingers. He lowered a wooden spoon covered in thick sauce back into the pan.

But Teeny was too excited to wait for a taste herself. She rushed to her bedroom and the large trash bag full of dog hair she had taken from her mom's grooming room.

Teeny pulled a ruler from her desk drawer. She used her dresser mirror to measure from one end of her top lip to the other. Three inches. Teeny clipped the same length of tape.

Teeny's stomach wriggled as if there were grub worms inside. *Would this work?* she wondered. Teeny plucked several bunches of cocker spaniel hair and patted them down evenly onto the tape. She sucked in a deep breath before smoothing the mustache onto her upper lip and looking into the mirror.

Teeny danced forward and backward, then side to side.

She, Teeny Sweeney, had just created the perfect business.

She thumbed through the binders and books on her desk until she landed on an unused picture album. Teeny carefully pulled off her mustache and pushed it onto one of the album's sticky pages.

After running to grab her backpack from beside the back door, Teeny flipped open her binder to that day's class notes. She began to answer all of Miss Powl's questions. The same questions that seemed so impossible to answer earlier took no time at all to answer now.

Had she created a product that people needed? Absolutely! Her brother had said so earlier that day. Teeny had a feeling boys everywhere would want to impress girls like Jen Lankton. But unlike her brother, they had money to spend. Unique idea? Check. Cost of production? Double check.

Clutching the bag full of dog hair, Teeny fell back on her bed. Forget not actually selling the product.

Teeny Sweeney would be rich!

Chapter 5

Let's Make a Deal

B y Monday, Teeny had an album full of mustaches. Thanks to her mom's booming grooming over the past three days, Teeny had curly, straight, brown, black—every type of mustache a customer might need. She'd worked all weekend. If it hadn't been for dinners at the table and church on Sunday, she probably would have never even left her room.

"So, kiddo, why are we here so early? Not that I'm complaining that you want to be at school for once." Mr. Sweeney pulled up to the steps of

Parker Elementary in his 55 Sides taco truck. He had worked just as hard as Teeny that weekend creating a new side called the Feisty Flave. It contained five different kinds of spicy peppers.

Mr. Sweeney turned to face Teeny in the backseat he'd had specially made so he could drive the kids around. Her dad was pretty much the best.

Teeny didn't have the usual time for chitchat. This was an unusual day. "I'm here for business today, Dad."

"What exactly does that mean? Does it have anything to do with why you were shut inside your room the past two days? The last time you were this focused on something, Garrett's mom had to shave his head."

Teeny slid open the side door. "I'm sorry, Dad, but that gum company claimed its gum was hair-stuck proof. That was a science experiment, really."

"Teeny..."

"Dad, it's fine. My business plan is about mustaches. Zane gave me the idea."

"Huh." Mr. Sweeney rubbed his own thick mustache. "That sounds like an interesting idea." He took the truck out of gear. "And harmless. See you this afternoon, sweet pea. Love you!"

Teeny nearly ran to the school's steps. Her dad's questions had wasted important money-making time. At least she already had the album out.

Instead of climbing the steps, she followed the sidewalk to the side of the school.

When Zane went to Parker Elementary— which was like, forever ago—the principal then, Principal Masterson, a former cellist in some bigwig orchestra, wanted to start an elementary orchestra. In order to fund it, he made deals with local shops and restaurants to advertise right outside the school. The parents threw a fit, saying they didn't want their kids staring at ads all day. The idea was dropped, but not before a

giant billboard was built, nearly taller than the school, and covered with an image of a giant bucket of chicken. A few years ago, a bad storm passed through town, knocking half the billboard down to the ground. So now, when kids had free time, they were there, throwing balls at what had come to be known as The Wall.

Monday was the only day of the week the PTA sold candy at lunch, and the entire school bought enough to last the week. Their pockets were already lined with Teeny's money, but the kids didn't know it yet.

Ten customers tossed a ball back and forth at The Wall, including Garrett and Jak Lee, the most popular kid in school. Normally, Teeny couldn't give a bump on a bullfrog's back about popularity, but today, she needed every boy at Parker Elementary to want a mustache. She needed Jak Lee.

"Hey." Teeny slipped her backpack to the ground. She held tight to the album that would

make her rich, ready to make her first pitch. But suddenly, Teeny thought of the end of a scripture in Psalms: "…though your riches increase, do not set your heart on them."

As quickly as the thought came, it vanished. Garrett had thrown a tennis ball hard against the billboard, and it pounded against the faded sun that smiled and winked at the bucket of chicken. "Hey, Teeny. You're here before the tardy bell? What gives?"

"Well, since you asked, I have a proposition for you." She motioned to all the kids in the courtyard. "For all of you, really."

Garrett opened his mouth, but Teeny shook her head slightly. He seemed to get the hint.

"Jak, you've had a crush on Sarah Price since first grade," Teeny said.

Jak gasped and began to choke on nothing. Garrett slapped him on the back until he stopped.

Jak fixed Teeny with a stare that would make a grizzly bear sweat. "That's not true."

Teeny refused to break eye contact. These kids would pounce on any weakness in less than a millisecond. "We all know it, and we all know she's a whole year older. So, it hasn't happened and probably wouldn't... until now."

Every kid stopped moving. Teeny patted her album. "A very trustworthy source told me that girls like facial hair. And I just so happen to have an album full of"—Teeny opened the album, flipping page after page—"fine mustaches."

As the kids stepped closer, the early morning chirps and car engine roars were replaced with *ooos* and *ahhs*.

All Teeny heard was a beautiful *cha-ching, cha-ching*.

Jak leaned back, folding his arms. "Okay. You've got my attention, Teeny Sweeney, but how much will they set us back?" He rubbed his fingers together. "I'm talking the green stuff: money."

Teeny slammed her album shut. "These mustaches are full of my blood, my sweat, my tears—"

"Gross!" Jak stepped back.

"Ewww!" Samantha Hayward squeaked.

"Seriously?" Teeny said. Patience was easier said than done. "Not my real blood, sweat and tears! I'm just saying I worked hard to make these beauties, and I didn't expect the first thing out of your mouth to be price."

Jak held up his hands. "Okay, okay. That was some nice-looking facial hair." He shifted his stance. "Now, what's the price?"

Teeny re-opened the album. She flipped through a few pages and then unstuck a sleek, dark mustache, courtesy of a schnauzer. Teeny gently placed it just above Jak's lip.

Everyone on the playground stared, but no one said a word.

Teeny dug a mirror from her bag. The grub worms in her stomach were eating her from the

inside out. She carefully held the mirror in front of Jak.

He stared silently. He ran his fingers over the full mustache.

And then, right in front of everyone, Jak Lee smiled, pulled a five-dollar bill from his pocket and asked, "Is this enough?"

Chapter 6

All in a Day's Work

Teeny Sweeney sold an entire binder full of mustaches by the end of lunch on the very first day she opened Sweeney's Staches. By the end of the day on Tuesday, she had sold a second  binder's worth that she had stayed up way too late creating the night before. And by Wednesday, every boy at Parker Elementary walked around the playground and the cafeteria like they owned the joint, their upper lips covered with full, handsome mustaches proudly on display.

For Teeny Sweeney, business had grown to a total of over six hundred dollars.

Garrett was now not only her best friend, but also her bodyguard. A girl couldn't be too careful when it came to cash.

"Make way. Make way." He held his arm out and ushered Teeny across the playground.

Jak Lee and Sarah Price walked, hand in hand, towards the monkey bars. Jak threw Teeny a nod on the way.

But not every third-grader was happy with Teeny's business. Amanda Mayweather glared from her perch on the small hill beside the tetherballs. Teeny pulled a wad of bills from the front pocket of her backpack. She used them to wave to Amanda, and then to fan herself. Amanda leaped from her spot and stomped down the hill. She pounded the closest tetherball.

"Only you could do this in three days, Teeny Sweeney." Garrett glanced from the slides to the

swing sets. Every mustache on the playground shone in its full glory, including his new red beauty.

"An honest three days' work, Garrett. An honest three days' work." Teeny pulled a five from her money fan and tucked it into her bodyguard's shirt pocket. "A little something for your troubles."

"Thanks, Teeny." Garrett's smile was far too big and far too goofy. He rubbed his fingers

across his sweet 'stache. "Where do you get your fake hair, Teeny? It's so soft."

Teeny shook her head, "You don't understand. It's actually—"

Before Teeny could explain, the end-of-recess bell rang. Every third-grader ran towards the school's doors. Everyone but Teeny; her backpack was too full of money.

Chapter 7

Easy Squeezy

Friday came faster than a kindergartener can stick a marble up his nose. Teeny wiped the recess dirt from her knees and sniffed her armpits. *Not bad*, she thought.

Amanda Mayweather did a movie star gasp and waved the air around her, as if she could smell Teeny from ten feet away.

If it had been any other day, Teeny might have needed to count to ten, but not today. Today she'd best her nemesis a different way, a way that wouldn't end in a call to Teeny's parents.

Amanda straightened the papers on her desk for the millionth time. Teeny choked down a laugh. She knew no matter how many times Amanda put her papers this way and that, for once Teeny had her beat. Teeny had actually run a real business and had made a cool profit of six hundred and fifteen dollars. Well, if she took away the six dollars for two new tape rolls, she'd made six hundred and nine dollars.

Amanda Mayweather having to watch her be adored by an entire class was worth even more than the cash.

A new scripture Teeny had learned in her Sunday school class, John 15:12, flashed into her brain: "My command is this: Love each other as I have loved you."

Teeny shook away the thought. There was no way that God meant for her to love Amanda Mayweather.

"Do we have any volunteers?" Miss Powl wore a bright yellow scarf, wrapped twice around her

neck. It was the same scarf she wore on the hundredth day of school, Career Day, and the day before Christmas break. It was her special scarf worn for special days. Just one more reason this would be a day carved in Teeny's brain forever.

Two hands reached for the sky: Teeny's and Amanda's.

The girls glared at one another. They were just a few cowgirl hats away from an old-fashioned showdown. Teeny squinted her eyes. She was about to spit when Miss Powl spoke. "Amanda, since your last name comes first in the alphabet, you may go."

Teeny swallowed her loogie.

Amanda scooted away from her desk. Hugging her papers tightly, she flipped her pigtail in Teeny's direction and walked to the front of the class.

"For my business, I would make and sell cheese." Amanda beamed.

Teeny had to hold back a gag.

"My cheese would be unique because of its key ingredient: goat's milk."

"Yuck!"

"Gross!"

"Barf-o-rama!"

More students laughed while others pretended to gag.

Teeny would have felt bad for anyone besides Amanda Mayweather. Miss Powl quickly shushed the rest of the class while Amanda continued her presentation.

Big tears welled in Amanda's eyes. She took a deep breath. "My family raises goats. My mom sells lotion and soaps at the farmer's market. She has never made cheese. I would sell my cheese at the farmer's market with my mom."

Amanda rattled on for another five minutes. Finally, she stopped.

"Thank you, Amanda. Your business plan was thorough and well researched. I would definitely purchase your cheese. Please turn in your papers."

"*Baaa!*" Someone from the back of the room did his best goat impression.

With her head lowered, Amanda placed her business plan on Miss Powl's desk and quietly returned to her seat.

"Okay, Tina, you're up." Miss Powl's eyes fell on the face of each and every student in the room. It was "the look" that both parents and teachers give when playtime has ended, when a kid shapes up or ships out, when the temperature seems to increase by a solid twenty degrees. "Unless you have an interesting question, please keep all comments to yourself."

Got it, Teeny thought, and she was pretty sure every other kid in Miss Powl's class got it too.

Teeny took her binder to the spot where Amanda had been only moments before. She blew the bangs from her eyes. "My business plan was Sweeney's Staches, as I think everyone knows by now."

Miss Powl covered her eyes. "So you're the reason for the mustaches, Tina?"

Teeny nodded.

"Tina, the assignment was a plan—not an actual business where you make money. Do you remember me saying that?"

Teeny nodded again.

Miss Powl uncovered her eyes. "Okay, then. Go on."

"Well, I saw a real chance to make money, so I took it." Teeny waited for Miss Powl's reaction. There wasn't one, so she continued. "For my business, I created mustaches. I got the idea from my brother Zane. He said girls like guys with facial hair. That was the need. I made a ton of money, because I created all the mustaches myself. My mom always just throws away the dog hair from her grooming business. So I used the leftover hair to make the mustaches. Easy squeezy, really."

The sound of fourteen third-grade boys ripping the mustaches from their faces was what

it must have sounded like if the biggest band-aid in the world had been ripped off a giant.

"Disgusting!" Garrett shouted.

"Teeny Sweeney!" Jak Lee yelled.

"What?" Teeny squished her face in confusion. The boys glared back at her, bright red rashes in place of their mustaches.

Teeny's eyes grew wide. "Oh."

Each boy turned to the other and began pointing.

"Your face. It's … not good," said Jak to Jason Womper.

"You're so red," said Garrett to Benjamin Carlson.

Miss Powl sat, scribbling for several moments. She then jumped up from her chair. "The projects will continue on Monday. I need to make copies of this letter to send home." She rushed to the door, calling over her shoulder, "Amanda, you're in charge."

And just like that Teeny had been beaten, once again, by Amanda Mayweather.

Teeny looked up at the ceiling and screamed. When she was finally done, she lowered her head and found her whole class staring at her as if she were Tommy Sullivan, the sixth-grader who stole all their lunch money. She had no idea how long they just sat there, scowling.

Finally, Jak Lee broke the silence. "What is wrong with you, Teeny?"

Teeny shook her head. "Nothing. It was a good idea."

"Good idea? You're crazy!" Winston Hempstead yelled.

Teeny looked to Garrett. He was her best friend, after all. Garrett's eyebrows sank lower than low. His voice came out just above a whisper. "How could you let me wear dog hair on my face all week, Teeny?"

"If I were you, Teeny, I wouldn't even think about showing your face at the fair tomor—" Jak's mouth shut tighter than a clam when Miss Powl rushed back through the doorway.

Everyone besides Teeny packed up and left the scene of the crime, taking a note from Miss Powl.

Teeny sighed. "I really thought it was a great idea." She stuffed the binder she never wanted to see again into her backpack.

Miss Powl touched Teeny's shoulder. "I know you did, Teeny."

Teeny jumped. It was the first time her teacher had ever called her anything besides Tina.

Miss Powl continued, "Something like that has to be tested and re-tested before it's actually sold, and customers are always made aware of the ingredients." Miss Powl sucked in a deep breath. "I will give you until around 4:30 pm, when I normally leave for the day, to tell your parents. I'll be calling them after that. Understand?"

Teeny's shoulders slumped as she nodded.

If her friends hated her, how would her parents feel?

Chapter 8

Ripple Effect

The 55 Sides taco truck stopped at the school's front curb. Both Mr. and Mrs. Sweeney waved from

their seats. It was unusual for both of Teeny's parents to pick her up.

The door slid open before Teeny could reach it. Zane nodded towards the empty seat by the window. "Hey, Teens." It was even more unusual for Zane to be with them.

Teeny climbed inside and dropped her backpack on the truck floor. Her dad turned to

the back from his driver's seat. "Hi, sweet pea. We're having tacos at our spot tonight. Yum, huh?"

Teeny nodded. They all seemed so happy, even Zane with his half-smile. She glanced at the truck's digital clock: 3:20. She had exactly one hour and ten minutes to spill a can of beans she *so* didn't want to spill.

The truck lurched forward, but not before Teeny caught Garrett's eye. He reached into his pocket and waved his dazzling red mustache high in the air. That was, until he threw it to the ground and stomped on the poor little fella over and over. And, without even looking back in Teeny's direction, her ex-best friend disappeared into the school bus.

Smiling, Mr. Sweeney turned to his two backseat passengers. "This evening, we are celebrating!" He squeezed Mrs. Sweeney's shoulder. "Today marks the one-year anniversary of your mother's Sweeney Sheen business.

We are celebrating her amazing and thriving accomplishment!"

Mrs. Sweeney actually blushed. If Teeny wasn't already sweating bullets, it might have been cute.

Minutes ticked away as Teeny's mom and dad shared stories of their days.

Mr. Sweeney had a record-breaking day, selling fifteen hundred tacos. He claimed it was his Feisty Flave. The cocker spaniel, Dixie, had taken home the first place trophy in the Parker City Pet Show. Mrs. Sweeney said it would be great advertising for her business. Even Zane had somehow scored a date with the famous Jen Lankton. She'd be accompanying him to tomorrow's fair.

At the word "fair," Teeny's insides crumbled. Jak's voice—"You better not even think about showing your face at the fair"—played over and over in her head, a horrible soundtrack to her horrible day.

It was 4 pm when they reached their favorite place, a pond just outside of the hustle and bustle of town. Weeping willow trees towered over the quiet waters, where ripples spread here and there, set in motion by curious fish or zigzagging bugs.

This was the Sweeney family's favorite place to be reminded of God's glory.

Teeny helped her father spread the red-and-white checkered tablecloth on the grass. They all carried over plates of her father's tacos and

pretty much anything a person might want to put on a taco. Even though there were so many options, Teeny always ate hers with just cheese and lettuce.

After praying, everyone dug in, except Teeny. Her mother's phone flashed 4:25.

"Is everything okay, Teeny?" Mrs. Sweeney asked.

Teeny inhaled and exhaled slowly. Her parents stopped eating. Even Zane's brows dipped. Her next words would surely ruin the rest of dinner, but she didn't have a choice.

"Do you remember my whole business plan?" Teeny's face grew hot. Burning lava hot.

Both parents nodded.

"Well, I may have made mine into more than just a plan."

"I'm pretty sure you mentioned that Miss Powl wanted a business in theory only. Right?" Teeny's dad said. His favorite spicy sauce dribbled down the side of his mouth. He was too interested in

what she said to wipe it away. Mrs. Sweeney handed him a napkin without taking her eyes off Teeny.

Teeny continued. "True, but there was a real need for my business. It would have been wrong to leave it just a plan."

"Go on, Teeny." Mr. Sweeney looked from his daughter to his wife. Both parents seemed to suddenly hold their breath.

"Anyway, there was a real need for facial hair at my school, so I created mustaches from Mom's leftover … dog hair … and I … sold them to all the boys at school."

Zane spewed cola all over the picnic blanket. Mr. Sweeney dropped his taco. Red sauce splattered across the otherwise spotless tablecloth. "You didn't, Teeny. Please tell me you did not sell mustaches made of dog hair to the boys at your school. Please tell me they did not wear dog-hair mustaches," her dad said.

"The little boys at your school were actually wearing dog hair on their faces this week?" Mrs. Sweeney pinched that tiny part just between her eyebrows and above her nose.

"Disgusting, Teeny!" Zane was laughing so hard, tears brimmed at the corners of his eyes.

Mr. Sweeney's phone made a sound like a doorbell. He sucked in two big breaths, letting the phone ring until Teeny's brain was so scrambled and her nerves were so shot, she was only two seconds away from grabbing the phone and making it fish food.

Finally, after one more long, grim look at Teeny, her father answered. "Hello … yes, I'm well. How are you, Miss Powl?"

Chapter 9

God Says So

Mr. Sweeney poured the final ingredient of his pecan pralines— the pecans themselves— into a medium-sized sauce pan.

The smell of the boiling butter, vanilla, and brown sugar mixture filled the kitchen. Such sweet smells could almost make Teeny forget that today was the absolute worst day of her life. Almost.

After Miss Powl's phone call, Teeny told her family all the hairy details, from Zane's need to impress Jen Lankton to what a horrible human

being Amanda Mayweather was, to the dog hair in the trashcan and The Wall and Jak Lee. She wrapped the whole, awful story up with that afternoon's presentation and how it went from amazing to dreadful.

By the time her story ended, the blue sky had grown a deep orange. No one spoke on the ride home. Teeny's mom said something about needing a quiet bath and Zane disappeared into his room. It was just Teeny and her dad mixing and stirring in silence.

"I'm sorry, Dad. I really am. I guess I should have followed Miss Powl's directions," said Teeny as she wrapped a praline in clear plastic and finished it with a bow for tomorrow's third-grade bake sale.

When the final bow was tied, Teeny's dad sat back and stared at her. "Okay, so here's the deal. I agree with Miss Powl about the plan staying a plan and you not running an actual business. She's right about products needing testing and

customers knowing what exactly it is they're buying. It was wrong and disrespectful to not follow her directions, and it was also wrong to focus all your attention on the money you were making. You were careless with the people that you love, and the people that God loves."

Teeny's throat did that whole aching like you may never speak again thing that it did anytime her parents were disappointed in her.

Mr. Sweeney paused. "However…"

Teeny straightened.

"Teeny, you're in third grade and you just ran your first business. You made over six hundred dollars in a single week! Yes, you have a lot to learn, but—" Mr. Sweeney blew out a low whistle. "Tina Michelle Sweeney, you are the tiniest entrepreneur I have ever known. My little business girl!" He leaned over and kissed Teeny's forehead.

Teeny wrapped every bit of her arms around her dad's shoulders. She needed him to say that and she didn't even know it.

Mr. Sweeney pulled two plates and two glasses from the cabinet. He poured two tall glasses of milk from the carton and slipped a pecan praline onto each plate. The sweet treat melted in Teeny's mouth.

"Dad, these are *sooo* good." She chased her treat with a big gulp of cold milk. "But it really doesn't matter if they're good or terrible. Jak Lee said I better not show up tomorrow, and I'm pretty sure every kid at Parker Elementary feels the same way."

Mr. Sweeney nodded. "They feel wronged, Teeny. They had no idea the mustaches were made of dog hair. Not to mention, they all now have rashes." Mr. Sweeney paused, seeming to really think about his next words. "You have to give all of them their money back."

"Dad, I put a lot of work into those mustaches. It's not fair."

Mr. Sweeney rubbed his daughter's back. "I know, Teeny, I know. However, it's not about what's fair to you, but what's the good and right thing to do for others. You sold your classmates a product that wasn't ready to be sold. No, they didn't ask what the mustaches were made of, but you never told them, either." He stopped and looked Teeny in the eyes. "What do you think is the right thing to do, sweet pea? "

Teeny peered up at her dad with tears trickling down her cheeks. "I guess the right thing would be to apologize to everyone and give them their money back, but I don't want to. It's going to be so hard."

"Do you remember what James 4:17 says? 'If anyone…' "

Teeny sighed. "knows the good they ought to do and doesn't do it, it is sin for them."

Mr. Sweeney stood and pushed his chair beneath the table. "Pray and ask God to help you. He will give you strength to do what you need to do. It might be hard, but I trust you to do what's right, sweet pea."

Teeny let her head and her tears fall on the table.

"And one more thing?" her dad said.

Teeny didn't look up. She didn't have the energy.

"God wants you to love *everyone*...even Amanda Mayweather."

Chapter 10

Tea Cups & Hurls

M r. and Mrs. Sweeney, Zane, and Teeny walked the grass path to the fair's entrance. A tall sign arched from one side to the other: *Welcome to Parker Fair.*

Teeny swallowed back the sour vomit taste creeping up her throat. She wasn't welcome here. She grabbed her dad's hand and tugged. "Please, Dad, let's skip the fair this year."

Mr. Sweeney put the box of pecan pralines on the ground. He crouched down to be eye to eye

71

with Teeny. "It'll be okay. Have I told you how proud I am of you today?"

Teeny smirked the tiniest of smirks and adjusted the straps on her bulging backpack. "At least twenty times."

But the happy moment didn't last long. "Dad, I've learned to pray. I know God speaks to us through scriptures and I know I have to make better choices. I've learned my lesson." She shrugged the backpack from her shoulders. "Can you please give everyone their money? They don't want me here. It's gonna be ugly."

A hand gently touched her shoulder. "Teens, did I ever tell you about the time my entire sixth grade class hated my guts over an accident?" Zane said.

"But you're like the most popular guy ever." She threw her hand to her hip. "Don't lie to me at a time like this, Zane."

"I'm not lying, Teens." Zane crouched and nodded towards the fairgrounds. "You know the giant tea cup ride?"

Teeny nodded.

"Well, when I was in sixth grade, my friends and I decided to ride it. Unfortunately, before we did, I thought it would be funny to hit signs with a couple rocks and my slingshot. My first shot missed a sign and instead, hit a bolt loose — the bolt that kept the tea cups from going too fast."

"No." Teeny's eyes grew wide.

"Yup. By the time a worker was able to stop the ride, most of my sixth-grade class, including me, had hurled our lunch all over the tea cups and each other."

Teeny fought down the vomit taste again. Two times in five minutes had to be a record. "Why are you telling me this right now? I'm already nauseous."

Zane slipped Teeny's backpack back on her shoulders. "I'm telling you this because, yes,

everyone was crazy mad at me. Crazy. Mad. But after a while, they got over it and everything was good."

Teeny sighed. "So you're saying everyone will get over it?"

"Bingo." Zane ruffled Teeny's brown curls. "In the meantime, maybe we could eat some ice cream or something. You know, when I'm not hanging out with Jen."

Teeny rolled her eyes, but her heart was secretly smiling. It was the first time in a really long time she'd seen *her* Zane. She punched him in the arm. "Maybe."

Teeny fixed her sights on the fair sign. *It's now or never,* she thought. She took her first step towards the hardest thing she had ever had to do.

Chapter 11

The Un-Fun House

Mrs. Sweeney giggled as she planted a small sign beside her husband's sweet creations. A bold purple arrow pointed to the rows of pralines. Above the arrow read: "I'm a delicious praline. Just saying."

Mr. Sweeney winked at his wife. They had the whole teamwork thing down.

Unfortunately, Winston Hempstead and Jason Womper were manning the third-grade booth, along with their parents. Two pairs of angry eyes

drilled the Sweeneys. The skin above both boys' lips was still as radish-red as it had been on Friday.

When the last praline was in place, Teeny's parents turned towards the rides and games. Winston and Jason pointed to the pralines and made gagging gestures.

Teeny felt like she had shrunk to the size of the ladybug that had just landed on the rock in front of her. She huddled closer to her parents. Her dad patted her shoulder and nodded towards her backpack. "Do you want us to help you with your task?"

She did. She really, really did, but she also didn't want her parents to miss out on a good time at the fair because of her. "No thanks. You guys have fun. How about you win Mom a goldfish or something?" Teeny plastered a big, toothy, fake smile on her face.

"Teens..." her parents said at the exact same time.

"No, guys. Have fun." She gave each parent a little push.

After one final look back, her dad wrapped his arm around his wife and they disappeared into the crowd.

Teeny dug two five-dollar bills from the pocket inside her backpack. She took a deep breath and turned back to Winston and Jason. "I'm sorry.

Here." She laid the money on the table in front of them.

Before waiting for their response, she hurried away. Two down, and about one hundred more to go.

In a matter of seconds, she had crossed paths with five more customers, all second-graders. They took their money, but the scowls remained.

Teeny spotted the fun house. This had always been her and Garrett's favorite thing to do at the fair. They'd make silly faces at each other in the crazy mirrors. A baseball-sized lump settled in her throat.

She fought back tears and entered the fun house by herself, but the goofy clowns, fog machine, and twisting tunnel just weren't the same. When she got to the mirrors, she wished she hadn't even gone inside in the first place.

As she stared at her reflection, several faces appeared behind her, all with bright red upper lips.

Jak Lee crossed his arms. "What are you doing here, Teeny Sweeney? I thought I un-invited you!"

"Yeah!"

"Scram, Teeny!"

The faces blurred as the tears streamed down Teeny's face. She threw her backpack from her shoulder and began to frantically dig inside. "Here! I'm sorry! I didn't mean for anything bad to happen. I'm really sorry!"

Hands reached for the green stuff, snatching it from Teeny.

"This still doesn't make everything good," Jak said.

"Hey, you heard her. She didn't know we'd get rashes. Cut her a break!" Garrett stepped from the group of third-graders and stood beside Teeny.

Teeny's broken heart thudded to life.

Benjamin Carlson stepped closer to Garrett. "Whose side are you on?"

Jak pulled Benjamin back. "They don't matter. The word's already out." Jak smirked.

"What do you mean the word's already out?" Teeny didn't like the way that sounded.

"I heard your dad made his pecan pralines this year." Jak walked closer to one of the fun house mirrors. He flattened a stray hair. "Too bad no one's going to buy any."

Teeny thought back to the night before and how hard her dad had worked on them. She stomped her feet on the wooden floorboards.

"Stop! Everyone just stop!" Someone stepped from the thick fog and into the flashing lights.

It was none other than Amanda Mayweather.

Chapter 12

The Last Person in the World

Teeny inhaled deeply, ready to yell, but Amanda shook her head. Teeny got the hint. She gulped down a mouthful of air.

"Did Teeny make some mistakes? Sure. But she's here, saying she's sorry and giving you your money back, isn't she? That's all she can do. What else do you expect from her?" Amanda walked to Garrett and Teeny.

"You know what I expect, A-man-da?" Jak said. "I expect this rash to go away, but it won't."

"If I can help with that, will you guys leave Teeny alone?" Amanda's voice was strong. She meant business. "And I mean for good. Everything would be just like it was before this mess."

The boys all looked at Jak. He nodded.

Amanda unzipped the fluffy dog purse strapped across her body. "Do you guys remember when I said my mom makes lotion?"

Benjamin backed away. "Ewww. What I remember is you said she makes it from goat's milk."

Amanda grabbed a dozen small tubes from her purse. "Go ahead. Leave if you don't want your rash to get any better."

Benjamin stopped.

"My mom has made and sold this lotion for years. She's actually really well known for it. This stuff will cure your rashes."

Every boy in the fun house grabbed a tube. They screwed off the lids and began to rub on the lotion. *Ooo*s and *ahhh*s filled the crazy mirror room.

Right away, Teeny could see their reddened skin lose some of its bright color.

The boys were nearly glued to the mirrors. Jak turned back to Amanda, smiling. "A deal's a deal." He pushed past Teeny. "Hey, let's go let the guys know those pecan pralines are back up for grabs."

What just happened? thought Teeny. "Ummm... you guys go on ahead. Meet ya there."

Everyone besides Garrett, Teeny and Amanda ran for the lighted exit.

Teeny turned to Amanda. "Why'd you do that?"

Amanda zipped up her purse and sighed. "I don't know. I guess I didn't want anyone to be mean to you. It didn't feel good the other day during my presentation, you know?"

Teeny's stomach plummeted to the floor. She did remember, and she also remembered she

didn't do anything to help. A verse from the Bible suddenly slid through her brain like the words on a neon sign you'd find in Times Square: "…In everything, do to others what you would have them do to you."

This is exactly what Amanda had done. She had treated Teeny like she wanted to be treated.

Teeny unbuckled the side of her backpack, and took out two carefully wrapped pralines. She left the backpack on the ground and wrapped one arm around Garrett's shoulder and the other around Amanda's—something she never thought she'd do. The pralines dangled close to her classmates' noses. "How about the three of us go and enjoy these extra pralines my dad made?"

Amanda and Garrett shook their heads. "How about we help you give everyone their money back first, Teeny?" Garrett said.

"And tubes of lotion." Amanda patted her dog purse.

"Okay, okay. But then we eat the pralines. Deal?"

Teeny's best friend for forever and her ex-enemy both agreed. Together, they walked towards the bright exit, with Teeny standing just a little bit taller than she had been when she entered.

Chapter 13

Beyond Measure

"And the class that made the most money at this year's bake sale is ..." Principal Turner paused for the row of kindergarteners to drum roll on the picnic tables.

The morning had grown into late afternoon, and the crowd was full of smiles and laughter.

"This stuff is amazing, Amanda." Garrett squeezed another dab of lotion onto his upper lip.

"Thanks. My mom worked really hard to perfect the ingredients. I'm glad it worked," Amanda said.

It was true. When Teeny looked around, all the boys' upper lips were now a dull pink.

Principal Turner continued, "…the third grade!"

Cheers rang through the crowd.

"Woo-hoo!"

"Yeah!"

"Sweet!"

The winning third-graders waited as Principal Turner and the parent volunteers passed out everything that makes up a banana split—cherries and all.

Zane nodded toward Teeny before walking to the cotton candy booth with Jen Lankton.

Teeny smiled. *I guess facial hair isn't a must, after all.*

Mrs. Sweeney dropped a scoop of vanilla ice cream into Teeny's bowl. She winked. "I'm proud of you, sweetheart."

Mr. Sweeney threw his daughter a thumbs-up from where he stood, passing out spoons to a group of eager students.

Teeny licked a swirl of whipped cream from her sundae. With her mouth full, she said, "That lotion is like magic. I can't help but wonder about the goat cheese you were rambling on about during your pres—"

"No!" Garrett shouted.

"But—"

"Let's talk ice cream today and business tomorrow. Deal?" Amanda dug in for a heaping spoonful of banana split.

Teeny laughed. The past week had been the wildest one of her life. And it had ended with some crazy business know-how, a new friend, and a better understanding of how God speaks.

Teeny Sweeney had indeed become rich.

★ It's No Secret... ♡

The new *Teeny Sweeney* series serves up a
**dollop of faith, a dash of fun,
and a sprinkle of mischief!**
Stay tuned for book 2 coming soon!

Book Club Questions for:

1. Teeny Sweeney is the main character of the story. Who was her best friend and who was the farthest thing from a friend at the start of the book? Did you like him/her?

2. If you invited Teeny Sweeney over to your house, what sort of activities would you enjoy doing with her?

3. What are three adjectives that you would use to describe Teeny to your friends?

4. Teeny's mom had a specific job. What was it? And, what did her dad, Mr. Sweeney, do for his job?

Teeny Sweeney and the Mustache Cash Written by Amberly Kristen Clowe, illustrated by Janet Samuel © 2018 Little Lamb Books / ISBN 978-0-9986243-6-5 / littlelambbooks.com

5. What was the setting of this story? How do you know?

6. What was the main problem Teeny faced in the story? How was it solved?

7. Miss Powl wore something special for important days in class. What was it? Do you have something that you wear when you have an important event?

8. What do you think is the lesson or moral of this story?

9. What new words did you learn? Make a list on a piece of paper of all the new words you discovered in the story.

10. If you could be friends with anyone (Teeny, Garrett, Amanda, Jak, etc.) in the story, who would you choose and why? Draw a picture of you and that character.

Teeny Sweeney and the Mustache Cash Written by Amberly Kristen Clowe, illustrated by Janet Samuel © 2018 Little Lamb Books / ISBN 978-0-9986243-6-5 / littlelambbooks.com

11. Was this book fiction or nonfiction? How do you know?

12. What was your favorite part of the story? What was your least favorite part of the story?

13. Would you recommend this book to your friends? Why or Why not?

14. What was your favorite Bible verse that Teeny learned in the story?

15. What kind of activities would you like to read about Teeny doing in the next book?

Teeny Sweeney and the Mustache Cash Written by Amberly Kristen Clowe, illustrated by Janet Samuel © 2018 Little Lamb Books / ISBN 978-0-9986243-6-5 / littlelambbooks.com

Getting to Know Teeny

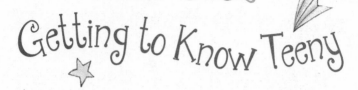

In *Teeny Sweeney and the Mustache Cash*, you meet Teeny Sweeney, a third-grader with a Dad, Mom, and big brother. She's determined to create the best business plan ever for her school assignment. Get to know Teeny better by unscrambling the words to reveal some of her favorites.

1. Favorite Month   NEUJ   ....

2. Favorite Food   COAT   ....

3. Favorite School Subject   TRA   ....

4. Favorite Season   MMUESR   ....

5. Favorite Fruit   WKII   ....

Teeny Sweeney and the Mustache Cash Written by Amberly Kristen Clowe, illustrated by Janet Samuel © 2018 Little Lamb Books / ISBN 978-0-9986243-6-5 / littlelambbooks.com

6. Favorite Animal   EEANTHLP ....

7. Favorite Color   PPLEUR ....

8. Favorite Holiday   HCIMRTASS ....

9. Favorite Instrument   MURSD ....

10. Favorite Dessert   EKAC ....

11. Favorite Flower   PLTIU ....

12. Favorite Vacation   GKISIN ....

Answers: 1. June 2. Taco 3. Art 4. Summer 5. Kiwi 6. Elephant 7. Purple 8. Christmas 9. Drums 10. Cake 11. Tulip 12. Skiing

Teeny Sweeney and the Mustache Cash Written by Amberly Kristen Clowe, illustrated by Janet Samuel © 2018 Little Lamb Books / ISBN 978-0-9986243-6-5 / littlelambbooks.com

Business Brainstorm

In *Teeny Sweeney and the Mustache Cash*, Teeny creates her own business from scratch for a class assignment. Have you ever thought about starting a business? If so, what would it be? A lemonade stand? A dog wash? A bakery? Answer the following questions about your business idea just like Teeny did, to create your first business plan. Remember, what Miss Powl said, "The sky is the limit".

Why do you want to start a business?
What's your idea?.......................................
....
....
Why is your business idea needed? ....
....
....

Teeny Sweeney and the Mustache Cash Written by Amberly Kristen Clowe, illustrated by Janet Samuel © 2018 Little Lamb Books / ISBN 978-0-9986243-6-5 / littlelambbooks.com

Teeny Sweeney: Business Brainstorm

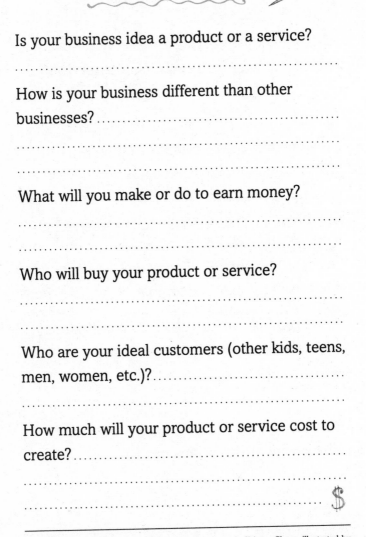

Is your business idea a product or a service?

. . . .

How is your business different than other businesses? . . . .

. . . .

. . . .

What will you make or do to earn money?

. . . .

. . . .

Who will buy your product or service?

. . . .

. . . .

Who are your ideal customers (other kids, teens, men, women, etc.)? . . . .

. . . .

How much will your product or service cost to create? . . . .

. . . .

. . . . $

Teeny Sweeney and the Mustache Cash Written by Amberly Kristen Clowe, illustrated by Janet Samuel © 2018 Little Lamb Books / ISBN 978-0-9986243-6-5 / littlelambbooks.com

Teeny Sweeney: Business Brainstorm

If customers are paying for a service, how much will it cost for you to complete the service?

....
....

Where will you sell your product or service?

....
....

How much will you charge for the product or service (sale price)?

....
....

What profit, or money, will you make (money you keep after you subtract your expenses)?

....
....

What name will you give to your business?
Is it unique or memorable?

....
....

Teeny Sweeney and the Mustache Cash Written by Amberly Kristen Clowe, illustrated by Janet Samuel © 2018 Little Lamb Books / ISBN 978-0-9986243-6-5 / littlelambbooks.com

How will you get the word out about your business? Online? Posters? Newspapers? Email?

. . . .

. . . .

What will you do with your earnings? Reinvest? Save for college? Donate? Shop?

. . . .

. . . .

. . . .

. . . .

Draw a picture of your business logo, label or sign.

Teeny Sweeney and the Mustache Cash Written by Amberly Kristen Clowe, illustrated by Janet Samuel © 2018 Little Lamb Books / ISBN 978-0-9986243-6-5 / littlelambbooks.com

HARRIS COUNTY PUBLIC LIBRARY
HOUSTON, TEXAS

❀ Author Acknowledgments

First, I would like to give you, the reader, a great, hearty *Thank You*. This book would not be possible without amazing readers like you. I am also beyond appreciative for Rachel Pellegrino at Little Lamb Books. No one works harder than this special lady, and I feel so blessed to get to go through each step of the publishing process alongside her. I am also incredibly grateful for the opportunity to work with my sensational editor, Lindsay Schlegel. She understood Teeny from the get-go and worked diligently to make this character and story even better for readers. Thank you, Janet Samuel, for bringing Teeny Sweeney to life with your gorgeous illustrations. I could never see her any other way now!

My heart is so full as I also thank my husband. Thank you for listening to my thoughts, laughing out loud at Teeny, praying for God's will, and being a true and sure encouragement. Finally, I absolutely must acknowledge my kids. Their brilliance and spunk and hearts of gold inspired many of Teeny's characteristics.

Bringing a story from a manuscript to a polished, published book really does take a village, and I'm privileged to call you all mine.

HARRIS COUNTY PUBLIC LIBRARY
HOUSTON, TEXAS

About the Author & Illustrator

Amberly Kristen Clowe is a veteran elementary school teacher who writes from her home in Texas with her husband, two children, and two dogs, Roxie and Bella. Amberly is an avid cycler and fan of all things coffee, and enjoys spending her days crafting stories that share faith in a fun way with young readers. *The Teeny Sweeney* series is her first chapter book series. Visit her at www.amberlykristenclowe.com.

Janet Samuel is a full-time illustrator with a bachelor's degree in illustrations from Swansea Metropolitan University. She lives in South Wales with her daughter, Alice, and her dog, Tilly, while focusing on work that is primarily aimed towards creative children's literature. She is represented by The Bright Agency.